YOU'RE FINALLY HERE!

Written and illustrated by Mélanie Watt

KIDS CAN PRESS

HOORAY!

YOU'RE HERE!

BUT WHERE WERE YOU?

LONG ENOUGH TO WATCH PAINT DRY ...

LONG ENOUGH TO FIND A NEEDLE IN A HAYSTACK ...

LONG ENOUGH TO LEARN AN ACCORDION SOLO ...

LONG ENOUGH TO GATHER DUST BUNNIES.

OOPS!

I GUESS WE GOT OFF ON THE WRONG FOOT.

Right foot →

HOORAY!

You're Here!

BUT SERIOUSLY,

WHERE WERE YOU?

YOU'RE HERE!

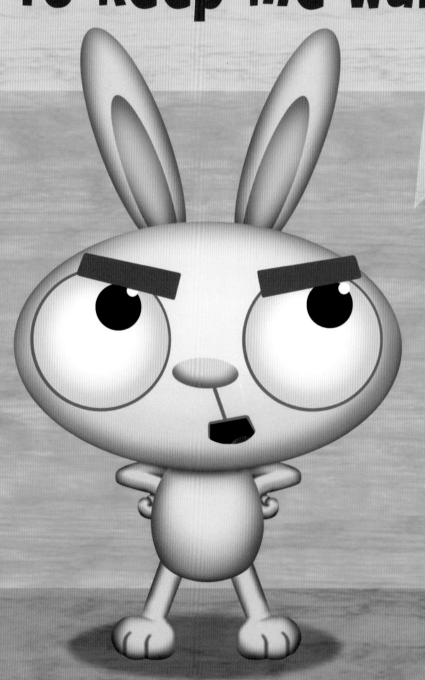

AS UNFAIR AS GETTING
PICKED LAST ...

AS UNFAIR AS HAVING TO GO TO BED
WHEN I'M NOT TIRED ...

AS UNFAIR AS HAVING TO EAT
A BRUSSELS SPROUT ...

AS UNFAIR AS BEING TOO
SHORT TO GO ON A RIDE.

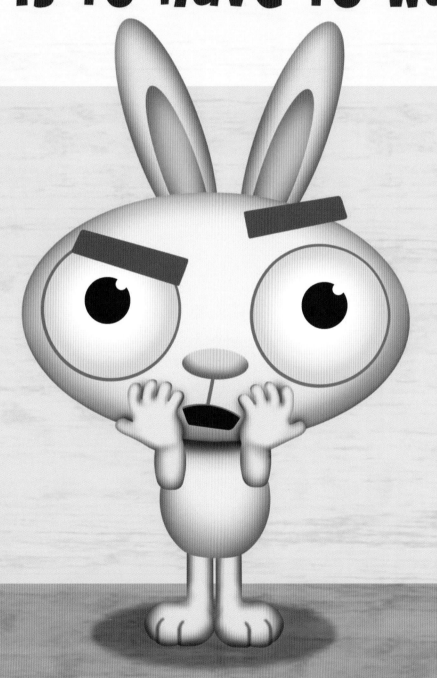

AS ANNOYING AS WEARING
AN ITCHY SWEATER ...

AS ANNOYING AS HAVING A SONG
STUCK IN MY HEAD ...

AS ANNOYING AS HAVING TOILET
PAPER STUCK TO MY FOOT ...

AS ANNOYING AS A PET ROCK.

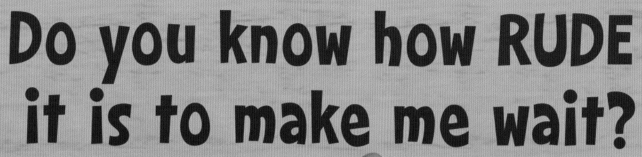

AS RUDE AS TALKING WITH
MY MOUTH FULL ...

AS RUDE AS STICKING
GUM UNDER THE SOFA ...

AS RUDE AS RUNNING ON CARPET
WITH MUDDY FEET ...

AS RUDE AS MAKING FACES
BEHIND SOMEONE'S BACK.

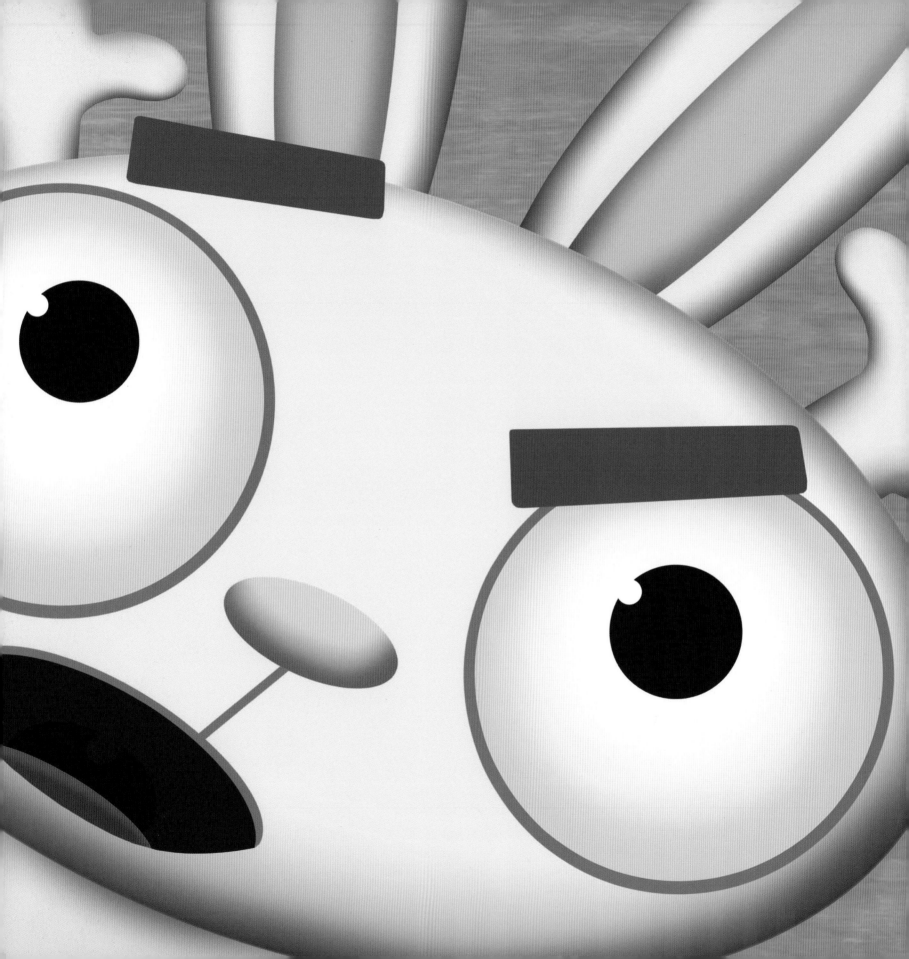

WHERE WERE YOU ALL THIS TIME???

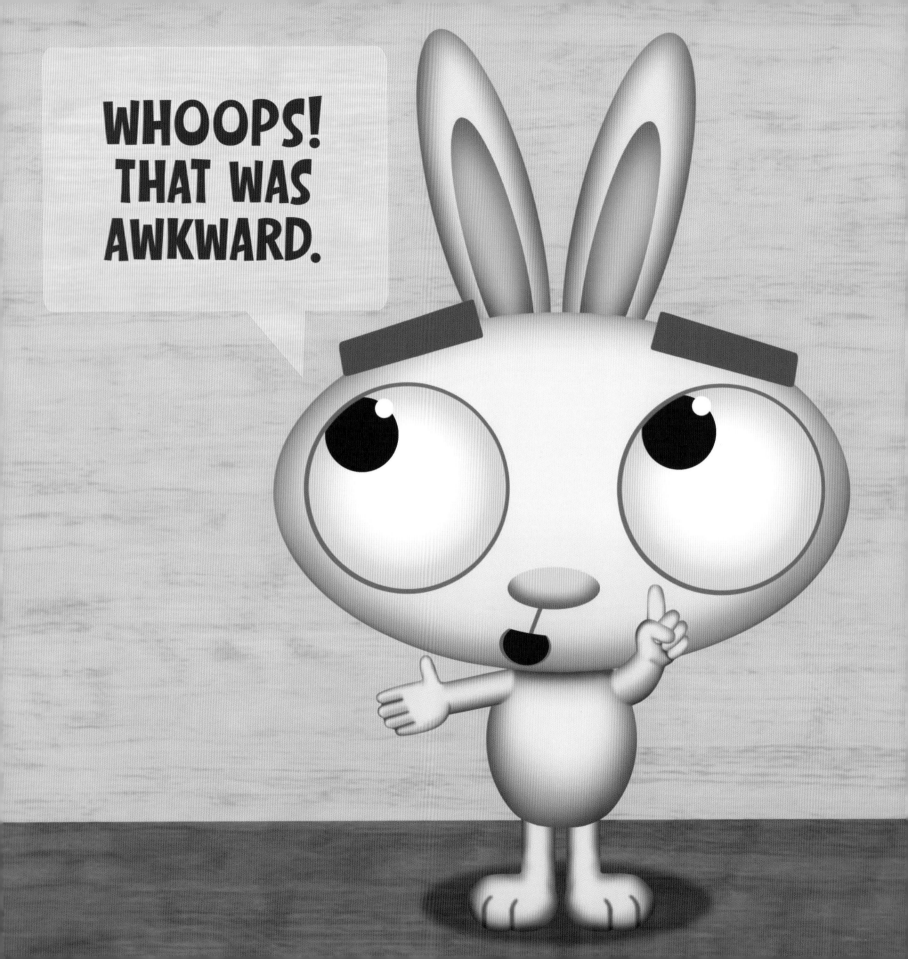

OKAY,
I PROMISE TO
STOP ASKING
WHERE YOU'VE
BEEN, IF YOU
PROMISE TO ...

-CONTRACT-

This document states that YOU, the reader, hereby agree to stay with ME, the bunny (book character of *YOU'RE FINALLY HERE!*), forever and ever. YOU, the reader, promise to devote all your attention exclusively to ME, the bunny. YOU, the reader, therefore agree never to keep ME, the bunny, waiting again!

And, oh yes, YOU, the reader, will provide ME, the bunny, with carrot treats every day.

_____
YOU, the reader

WAIT.
Hold
that
thought.

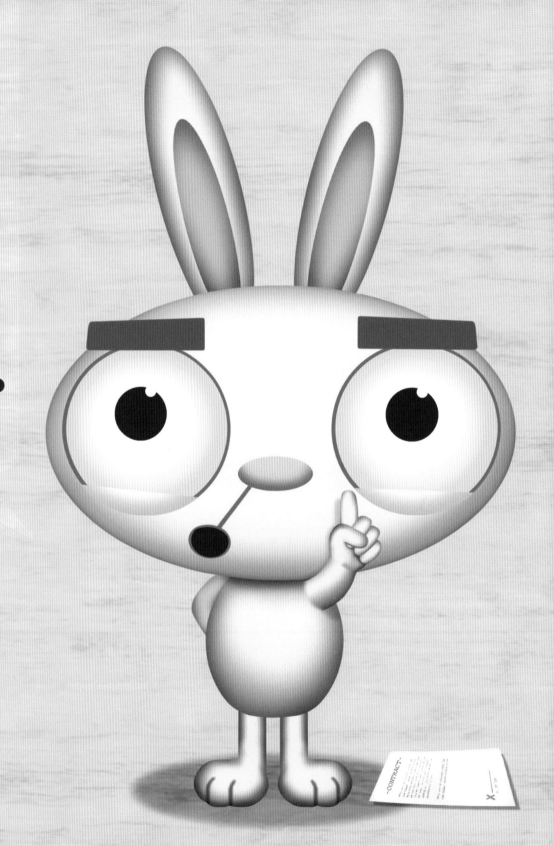

For Delphine, Ophélie, Annick and Jean-Seb

Kids Can Press gratefully acknowledges the financial support of the Government of Ontario, through the Ontario Media Development Corporation; the Ontario Arts Council; the Canada Council for the Arts; and the Government of Canada, through the CBF, for our publishing activity.

Published in Canada by Kids Can Press Ltd.
25 Dockside Drive, Toronto, ON M5A 0B5

Kids Can Press is a Corus Entertainment Inc. company

www.kidscanpress.com

Printed and bound in Shen Zhen, Guang Dong, P.R. China, in 12/2018 by Printplus Limited

CDN 11 0 9 8 7 6 5 4

Library and Archives Canada Cataloguing in Publication

Watt, Mélanie, 1975–
    You're finally here! / Mélanie Watt.

ISBN 978-1-55453-590-3

I. Title.

PS8645.A884Y68 2011   jC813'.6   C2010-905529-2

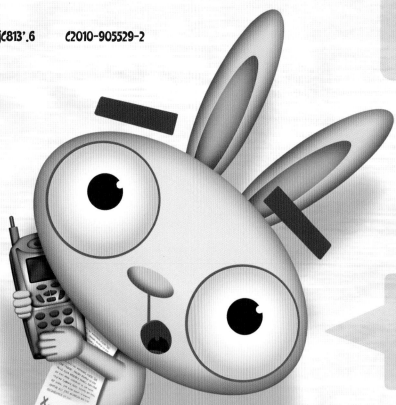